STICK DOG

DREAMS OF ICE CREAM

Praise for the STICK DOG series

"Full of silly, slapstick doggy humor.

An enticing package."

—*Kirkus Reviews*

"Readers are sure to enjoy this adorable story

about working together toward a goal."

—ALA *Booklist*

"Will be a sure hit with children."

—*School Library Journal*

STICK DOG

DREAMS OF ICE CREAM

By Tom Watson

HARPER
An Imprint of HarperCollins*Publishers*

Dedicated to Carol, Donna, Susie, Richard, Jim, and Tom

Stick Dog Dreams of Ice Cream

Copyright © 2015 by Tom Watson

Illustrations by Ethan Long based on original sketches by Tom Watson

All rights reserved. Printed in the United States of America.

No part of this book may be used or reproduced in any manner whatsoever without written permission except in the case of brief quotations embodied in critical articles and reviews. For information address HarperCollins Children's Books, a division of HarperCollins Publishers, 195 Broadway, New York, NY 10007.

www.harpercollinschildrens.com

Library of Congress Cataloging-in-Publication Data

Watson, Tom.

Stick Dog dreams of ice cream / by Tom Watson ; illustrations by Ethan Long. — First edition.

    pages cm. — (Stick dog)

"Illustrations by Ethan Long based on original sketches by Tom Watson."

Summary: Stick Dog and his feral friends are looking for relief on a very hot day—and this time they have their eyes on a ice cream truck.

ISBN 978-0-06-227807-4 (hardcover) — ISBN 978-0-06-300689-8 (pbk.)

1. Feral dogs—Juvenile fiction. 2. Dogs—Juvenile fiction. 3. Ice cream, ices, etc.—Juvenile fiction. 4. Friendship—Juvenile fiction. 5. Humorous stories. [1. Dogs—Fiction. 2. Ice cream, ices, etc.—Fiction. 3. Friendship—Fiction. 4. Humorous stories.] I. Long, Ethan, illustrator. II. Title.

PZ7.W3298Su 2015   2014030713

[Fic]—dc23   CIP

                                                                                        AC

Typography by Tom Starace

21 22 23 24 25   PC/LSCH   10 9 8 7 6 5 4 3 2 1

❖

First Edition

TABLE OF CONTENTS

Chapter 1

ESCAPE FROM THE HEAT

It was really, really hot.

Stick Dog, Stripes, and Poo-Poo looked forward to some brief relief from the heat.

And Mutt was just back from the creek to provide it.

He was sopping wet. He didn't say anything
at all but simply sidled up close to the others.
They all knew the routine. This was, after all,
Mutt's fourth trip to the creek in the past
hour. Stick Dog, Stripes, and Poo-Poo stood
at the ready.

And then Mutt began to shake. He started
slowly at first, spraying the others with big
droplets of water from his shaggy fur. But
then his shaking sped up, until he trembled
and vibrated so
hard the dry dirt
around his paws
puffed up in little
brown clouds.
With this vigorous
shaking, Mutt was
able to spray his

companions not with big droplets of creek water but with a fine, cooling mist.

The other three sighed as they felt the wet, cool relief.

"That feels wonderful," whispered Stripes when Mutt finally stopped shaking.

"I never get tired of that smell," Poo-Poo said.

Stick Dog enjoyed the temporary respite. He needed a little break from the dry, hot day as much as anyone. "Thank you again, Mutt. That really does feel great," he said. "Come on, you guys. Let's help him retrieve some of this stuff. That's the least we can do."

Immediately, Poo-Poo and Stripes helped Stick Dog gather all the things that had come flying out of Mutt's fur with the water. They picked up a crushed Ping-Pong ball, a blue marker, two bottle caps, and an old gray sock. They returned them all to Mutt, who tucked everything back into his fur except the old gray sock. He took that to the shade of a beech tree and began to chew on it.

Poo-Poo and Stripes shared some shade under an old oak tree. And Stick Dog settled beneath a leafy maple. Unlike Mutt's shaking, the shade provided little help. They all heated up again quickly.

"Stick Dog," Poo-Poo said. "We have *got* to do something about this heat."

"There's not much we can do," Stick Dog answered. He seemed to be conserving his energy as he spoke. He didn't even turn to address Poo-Poo. "My pipe is even warmer than out here. The air doesn't circulate in there. We're not going to find better shade anywhere. I guess we could go down to the creek and get another drink of water. That always helps a little."

"I'm sick of drinking creek water," Stripes said. She sounded frustrated. "It's too sandy and gritty. And on a day like this, it's not even cold."

"Let's go look for some new water," suggested Mutt. "Maybe we can find a better place to get it."

Stick Dog considered this. "A new water source, hmm? Cleaner, colder. I think it's a good idea."

"You do?" said Mutt. "Really?!"

Stick Dog nodded. "Let's just wait for Karen to get here and then we'll go look."

"Did you hear that, you guys?" Mutt asked Poo-Poo and Stripes. There was genuine excitement in his voice. "Stick Dog thinks we should go find a new place to get water. It was my idea! Did you hear me suggest that?"

Poo-Poo nodded his head, and Stripes closed her eyes.

"Another great idea by yours truly," Mutt whispered to himself as he shifted around a little in the shade. "Old Mutt comes through again."

Stick Dog took pleasure in seeing Mutt act this way. And he took even greater pleasure when a random summer breeze whooshed through the woods for a few seconds. He closed his eyes and waited for Karen.

He didn't have to wait long.

Chapter 2

GOING NOWHERE

Karen soon came through the woods and entered the small clearing at Stick Dog's pipe. She joined him beneath the maple tree.

"Can you believe how hot it is?" Karen said as she plopped down.

"Don't remind us," sighed Stripes.

"Where have you been?" Poo-Poo called from beneath the oak tree.

"Nowhere," Karen answered. She panted and added, "It's so hot!"

"I said, 'Don't remind us,'" Stripes complained. She seemed really agitated. "And you can't be 'nowhere.' That's impossible."

Poo-Poo nodded in agreement.

Mutt ignored the entire conversation. He had now chewed through the heel of the old  gray sock and was working on the toe area.

"Look," Stripes said to Karen. "You don't have to tell us where you've been. It's your business. But you have to agree that you can't go 'nowhere.'"

"Yeah," Poo-Poo said. "You have to admit that."

Karen's chin rested on the ground. She didn't respond, but she did shift her eyes to look at Stick Dog next to her. It was almost as if her eyes were saying, "I really want to prove these two wrong, but I don't know how. Can you help me?"

Stick Dog got the message. And he thought it was just too hot for this back-and-forth conversation. On a nicer, cooler day, it would be fine—maybe even amusing. But not today. Not in this heat.

"Listen, Stripes and Poo-Poo. Do me a quick favor, will you?" Stick Dog asked. He stood and stretched his legs. He knew they would leave soon. "On the count of three, will you two go and climb into my pipe? It's not a race or anything. I just want you to get into my pipe for a second. Okay?"

It was an odd request, but neither Poo-Poo nor Stripes saw any harm in doing so. They nodded to indicate they would do it.

"One, two . . . ," Stick Dog said, and then paused. He waited. Poo-Poo and Stripes were ready to move from the oak tree's shade to Stick Dog's pipe, but they held still, waiting for the signal. Then Stick Dog said, "Forget it. I don't want you guys to go to my pipe after all."

"You don't?" asked Stripes.

Stick Dog shook his head.

"Why not?" Poo-Poo asked.

"Just changed my mind is all," said Stick Dog. He winked at Karen and turned to Stripes and Poo-Poo. "Can I ask you both a question?"

They nodded.

"Where did you guys go?"

Stripes looked at Poo-Poo. Poo-Poo looked at Stripes. They both looked at Stick Dog, shrugged their shoulders, and answered together, "Nowhere."

"Yes!!" Karen exclaimed, and began hopping up and down. "I knew Stick Dog could prove it! I knew he could! You two just went 'nowhere'!"

"Wait a minute, wait a minute," Stripes began to complain.

"That's not right. That's like word magic or something," Poo-Poo said, and shook his head. "That's what it is: word magic."

Stripes turned to Mutt, hoping that he could help them. She called over, "Mutt, what do you think about all this?"

Mutt lifted his head. The other dogs were too far away to see it, but gray and white threads hung from the corner of his mouth. He seemed to take the question very seriously. He tilted his head a bit to the left as if pondering something that concerned him quite deeply.

"Well, what do you think?" Stripes called again.

"I think," Mutt said, "that was the best darn sock I've ever eaten."

Stick Dog smiled and said to them all, "Come on. Let's go find some nice, cold water."

Karen followed Stick Dog with light, happy, and energetic steps.

Poo-Poo and Stripes followed as well— glad to end the conversation.

And Mutt came along too. He was eager to find something to help wash down the final threads of that old gray sock.

Chapter 3

POO-POO IS QUITE SPECIAL

Halfway through the forest, Poo-Poo skidded to a halt. He snapped his head left and right, up and down. He sniffed continuously as he jerked his head all around. The other dogs had all slowed and stopped to watch this display.

"What is it, Poo-Poo?" asked Mutt. "Do you smell something?"

"Oh, I smell something, all right," Poo-Poo

declared. He inched closer to a large oak tree. "I just can't put my paw on it. But it smells familiar."

"Is it hamburgers?" asked Karen with real hope in her voice.

"Or frankfurters?" asked Stripes.

"Maybe pizza?" Mutt asked.

Poo-Poo answered all three questions by shaking his head. "Up in the tree," he whispered as he stepped quietly toward the big oak's trunk. "Squirrel."

This is what Stick Dog was afraid of. He knew that Poo-Poo could stalk a squirrel for hours. And it was too hot—way too hot—to be delayed by this.

Poo-Poo circled the tree a few times, stopped, and peered up through the leaves and branches. He took a couple of short, quick sniffs. "There's a fuzzy-tailed, acorn-munching chatter-mouth up there, all right," Poo-Poo whispered. "If I could see him, I'd get him."

"Can't you see him, Poo-Poo?" Karen asked.

He shook his head but kept peering up into the top branches.

"Then how do you know there's a squirrel up there?" asked Stripes.

"Are you kidding me?!" Poo-Poo exclaimed, taking real offense. "I can smell a barbecue potato chip three miles away. I can smell a smoking grill in the next county. I can

distinguish whether a tortilla chip in a garbage can on the other side of Picasso Park is nacho cheese flavor or cool ranch flavor. You think I can't sniff out a nasty, nutty-breathed tail-shaker?!"

"Okay, okay," said Stripes.

Mutt didn't pay much attention at all. He was twisting his tongue around inside his mouth trying to get the sock strings dislodged from between his teeth.

Sorry. I just need to interrupt the story here for a minute—because this thing that's happening to Mutt drives me crazy too.

You probably remember from the previous stories that I need to make little comments here and there sometimes. I can't help myself. And, umm, you're not going to hassle me about it, right?

Thanks.

Anyway, I can't stand that feeling of having something stuck in my teeth.

Worst food for getting stuck in your teeth? Celery.

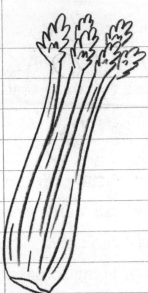

I love celery. It's crunchy and tastes pretty good for, you know, a vegetable. Dip it in a little peanut butter, and you almost forget that you're eating something healthy and green.

But it's the worst for getting stuck between your teeth. It's kind of stringy to begin with, and those strands have a special way of getting stubbornly stuck. And here's the worst part: they're a little bit slimy because the spit in your mouth combines with the moisture in the celery, and that makes the stringy parts impossible to grab. Believe me, I've tried. I've shoved my whole hand in my mouth trying

to get a celery
strand out. I grip
it real good and
then—SLIP!—I
can't get it.

It's super
annoying.

So I can totally relate to what Mutt's trying
to do here with the strings from that old
gray sock. While he did his best to get those
strings out, Poo-Poo continued to circle the
tree trunk as he stalked the squirrel. Karen
and Stripes had found some shade several
steps away, where they settled in to observe
the whole affair.

"That sneaky, sniveling villain," Poo-Poo muttered to himself when he stopped once to glare up into the tree for a moment. "If I could just get my paws on him, then I—"

"Poo-Poo?"

It was Stick Dog.

Poo-Poo jerked around for a moment, surprised out of his squirrel-stalking trance. He snapped his head toward Stick Dog and then yanked it back around to stare up into the tree again. "Yes, Stick Dog?"

"I don't mean to interrupt you here," Stick Dog began. "And if I'm ruining your concentration or something, just tell me and I'll stop bothering you."

"It's no problem. I can do more than one thing at a time. I can circle the tree while we talk," Poo-Poo said confidently. He proceeded to pace again. In just a couple of steps, he stubbed his front right paw on a tree root, stumbled, and rammed his shoulder into the tree trunk, knocking off a big chunk of brown-and-black bark. "Go ahead, I'm listening."

"Well, I was just thinking about what you said a couple of minutes ago," Stick Dog commented. "About how you can smell things from really far away? Like the flavor of a tortilla chip across the park or a grill from a long way away?"

"Mm-hmm, that's right," Poo-Poo said. He nodded his head at Stick Dog, and this seemed to throw him off balance again. He hit his head against the tree. Poo-Poo rubbed it, smiled, and before continuing to circle, whispered to himself, "Just like old times."

Stick Dog allowed Poo-Poo to regain his footing before he asked, "But can you smell *water*?"

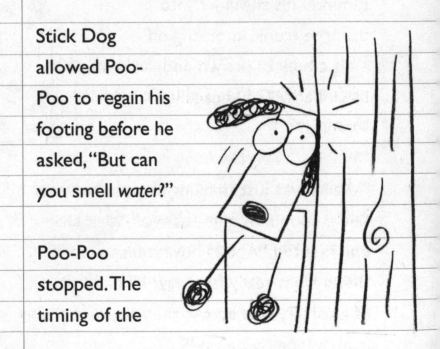

Poo-Poo stopped. The timing of the

question came just when he was on the opposite side of the trunk from Stick Dog. He didn't move his body but did stretch his neck out and around the tree to look directly at Stick Dog. "I can smell anything, anywhere, anytime," he said with absolute confidence. And then, with increased emphasis, he added, "I'm Poo-Poo."

Stick Dog pressed his lips together and nodded his head in full understanding. He then came closer to the tree. By this time, the heat had made Stripes and Karen feel drowsy. They were both lying in the shade with their eyes closed. Mutt did the same, but every now and then you could see his tongue press his cheek out as he probed around to get the sock strings out from his teeth. None of them were close enough to hear Poo-Poo and Stick Dog.

"I don't want to embarrass the others," Stick Dog whispered, and nodded toward Stripes, Karen, and Mutt. "But I think you might be the only one here who can smell water. And I'm not sure the four of us can find any cold water without your refined and ultra-sensitive sniffing capabilities."

Poo-Poo nodded and whispered back, "I see. Yes. I am quite special."

Stick Dog nodded and continued in the same hushed tone. "Without your help, we might be in danger. It's awfully hot. And we're all awfully thirsty."

Poo-Poo nodded again in understanding. "You guys might not stand a chance without me."

"That's right. It's all up to you," Stick Dog whispered. "You can stay here and try to get the squirrel. Or you can come with your friends, who are in desperate need, and help us find something to drink."

Immediately, Poo-Poo cleared his throat.

When he did, Stick Dog backed away, and the other dogs all opened their eyes.

"I have an announcement," Poo-Poo declared loudly. "Despite the fact that my arch-nemesis resides somewhere in the branches above me, I have decided to leave this place. I'm quite certain that it would only be a few minutes before I figured out a way to corral this tail-twitching nuisance. But those are minutes I choose to forfeit so I can use my expert sniffing abilities to deliver my friends from thirst and anguish."

Poo-Poo lifted his head and took a great and authoritative snort. He turned in several directions, sniffing and pondering. Finally, he pointed with his nose and said, "There is water this way! Follow me, my dry-mouthed comrades!" Poo-Poo then ran off into the forest.

By this time, Mutt, Karen, and Stripes had sauntered up to Stick Dog. They all had puzzled looks on their faces.

"Stick Dog?" Karen asked.

"Yes?"

"Didn't Poo-Poo just run off in the exact same direction we were going before he stopped to look for the squirrel?"

Stick Dog thought for a moment before answering. "Yes. Yes, he did."

And off they ran.

Chapter 4

RUNNING AROUND IN UNDERWEAR

It only took a couple of minutes for Stick Dog, Stripes, Karen, and Mutt to catch up with Poo-Poo, who was running with his nose slightly elevated through the woods. And it was only a few minutes after that when they all reached the other side of the forest. They stopped to survey their surroundings from behind a couple of big logs.

They could see the backs of four houses. Between them and the houses were four good-sized yards. Each yard had something different in it. From left to right, the first yard had a swing set, the second had a patio with some furniture, and the third had a badminton net.

But it was the fourth yard that caught the attention of all the dogs—except for Poo-Poo.

You see, in the fourth yard, three small humans were running in, out, and around a water sprinkler.

"Stick Dog," said Mutt, "I think that funny machine is spraying wat—"

Quickly, Poo-Poo interrupted. "Shh!" he said loudly. His eyes were closed, and his head swayed back and forth in a rhythmic, almost hypnotic pattern. "I'm sniffing for water."

"But if you just look over—" Mutt started to explain.

"Quiet. Please. I'm trying to work,"
demanded Poo-Poo. He crossed his hind
legs and went into a meditative position. He
then whispered, "I am becoming one with
the smells."

"But all you have to do is open your—"
Stripes began, but she was interrupted by
Poo-Poo as well.

"Really, I must insist," he said. There was no
meanness in his voice, but you could tell he
took his water-finding role very seriously.

Mutt, Karen, and Stripes all looked at Stick
Dog. They opened their eyes wide and
pointed toward the water sprinkler.

Stick Dog said nothing. He simply nodded
his head in recognition and raised his right
front paw calmly. Together they waited
patiently for Poo-Poo to finish.

In a moment, he did. Poo-Poo lowered his
head, opened his eyes, and then turned

directly toward the yard where the little humans played in the sprinkler.

"There!" he said triumphantly, and pointed. "I have smelled out our new water source. It's over there!"

Stripes, Mutt, and Karen just looked at Poo-Poo with blank expressions on their faces. They truly didn't know what to say.

"I know, I know," Poo-Poo said, and smirked a little in an attempt at modesty. "It's hard to understand, I know. I just have a talent for smelling out solutions like this. I can't help it.

It's just a gift, I guess. Sometimes I can't even believe the things I do myself."

Stripes, Karen, and Mutt still did not know what to say.

So Stick Dog spoke up. "Sometimes, Poo-Poo, I can't believe the things you do either," he said. And then he added, "Great job."

Karen turned away from Poo-Poo and toward Stick Dog and asked, "How are we going to get to the water? Those little humans are all over it."

"What are they doing with it anyway?" asked Stripes.

"I'm not sure," answered Stick Dog. "Let's get a closer look. Stay by the forest line."

Mutt, Poo-Poo, Karen, and Stripes followed Stick Dog along the edge of the woods. They snuck behind sticker bushes, cattail reeds, and tall, thick weeds. Soon they were staring out from behind a neatly stacked pile of logs.

They stared for a few minutes without saying anything as the three small humans

darted in and out of the spraying water. Safely concealed behind the woodpile, the dogs gathered around Stick Dog after this brief period of observation.

"Okay, what are we looking at here?" he asked.

Karen spoke first. "It's raining up from the ground," she said confidently and without hesitation. She motioned with her paws to demonstrate how the water rose up from the ground. "I believe somehow a small storm cloud has crashed into the earth in that yard. During the crash, it flipped over and is now raining up instead of down."

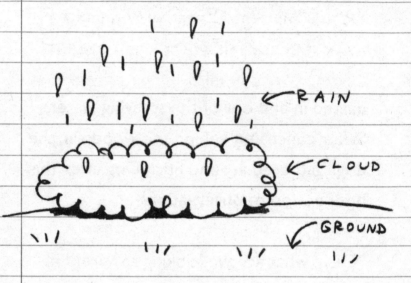

"All right," said Stick Dog slowly.

"Yes, that makes sense," Mutt said. He was kind of mumbling because he was still poking his tongue between his teeth to dislodge the strings from that old gray sock. "Upside-down rain cloud. That's it for sure."

"I don't think that's true," said Stripes, who had another idea altogether. "I think the water is actually attacking them. Just look at it! It's shooting all over the place trying to get them. And those little humans seem awfully frightened by it. They keep running up to it and then running away from it over and over again. Yep, it's definitely a water-attacking machine of some sort."

Stick Dog looked through some of the cracks and cavities in the woodpile. The little humans were, in fact, doing exactly what Stripes described. But he didn't think they looked very scared at all.

This is when Poo-Poo spoke up.

"These are not normal little humans," Poo-Poo said. "They're afraid of water, and they run around in their underwear. They're bizarre—even for humans."

Stick Dog looked through the woodpile again. He saw one of the small humans walk to the side of the house and turn a knob. When he did, the water stopped spraying. After they each grabbed a towel from the grass and dried off, the humans went inside the house.

"See? I told you they were a strange bunch," said Poo-Poo. "Why would you want to dry off on a day like this? The wetter, the better, I say."

"Hey, where'd the water go?" asked Mutt.

Karen shrugged her shoulders. "Stopped raining, I guess."

Stick Dog backed away from the woodpile

and addressed the others. "I don't think it's actually a rain cloud, and I don't think it attacks. It could be some kind of machine, though," he said. "Let's wait just a minute to make sure they're not coming back out. Then we can run in and get something to drink. I'm sure there are still some nice-sized puddles there."

The others nodded along with this idea—and got ready to run.

Chapter 5

A WATER MACHINE ATTACKS

They sprinted out of the woods and into the yard. They lapped at several small puddles in the grass.

There were not as many puddles as they hoped. They were small in size too. And they were absorbed quickly by the ground—and evaporated by the heat of the day.

"I think you were right, Stripes," Karen said as she paced around looking for a puddle. She noticed the mechanical nature of the sprinkler. "I think it is a water-attacking machine."

Stripes was too busy drinking from a small puddle that was quickly disappearing to say anything, but she did nod and smile. She was glad to be correct.

Stick Dog smiled too. He said, "I'm just glad it's not attacking now."

When the few puddles were gone, Stripes

and Mutt licked at the sprinkler itself as it continued to drip and bubble refreshing, cold water. Karen and Poo-Poo saw this and tried to nudge themselves in for a drink too.

Stick Dog stood back. He noticed that his friends were bumping and shoving more than they were actually drinking. There was really only room for two dogs at a time.

"Karen, Poo-Poo," he called.

They lifted their heads. This gave Mutt and Stripes ample room to continue drinking these few new drops in comfort.

"What is it, Stick Dog?" Karen asked.

"Follow that long, green tube that's connected to this water machine," Stick Dog said, and pointed. "It goes all the way to the side of the house. It looks like it's dripping over there too."

This is exactly what Poo-Poo and Karen did. And even though they could see the end of the hose attached to the faucet at the side of the house, Karen and Poo-Poo did not run in a straight line to it. Instead,

they lowered their heads and followed the
hose along its path in the grass. It twisted
and turned and looped all over the yard.
When the two of them ultimately reached
the side of the house, they were happy to
discover water dripping where the hose
connected to the spigot. This outside
faucet dripped a single drop of water
every second or two.

KAREN & POO-POO'S PATH

Karen and Poo-Poo took turns lying on
their backs. They opened their mouths and

let the cool, clear water drip in. It tasted terrific, but it was an awfully slow process. Poo-Poo needed to keep his mouth open for nearly a minute just to get a full swallow. And for Karen, who had a much smaller mouth, it still took nearly thirty seconds.

After a couple of turns each, Karen got an idea. She came closer to the spigot handle.

"Poo-Poo," she said. "Can you look at this for a minute?"

After getting a mouthful of water and swallowing it, Poo-Poo stood up and came

next to Karen. "What is it?"

"I think this thing might control the water drips."

They both stood there at the faucet for several seconds, tipping their heads left and right in thought.

"If it's dripping a little, maybe we can make it drip a lot," suggested Poo-Poo. "Maybe if you move it, some more water will drip out."

This made sense to Karen, and she nudged her nose against the faucet handle. It moved a half inch or so around, and it did indeed produce the desired effect there at the house. The drips came a little bit faster, but still not enough to provide a great thirst-quenching drink.

"It sort of worked," Poo-Poo observed.

"Yeah, sort of."

"Maybe you should move it some more," said Poo-Poo.

Karen shrugged her shoulders and said, "Sure, why not?"

She pressed her nose against the faucet again, but this time it didn't move. She pressed a little harder, and it still didn't move. She pulled her head back a couple of inches and bumped the faucet handle. It still didn't budge. "It's stuck," she declared.

"Stuck, huh?" Poo-Poo said, and backed several steps away. "We'll see about that."

Poo-Poo lowered his head, tightened his shoulder muscles, and took six quick strides forward, bashing his head directly into the faucet. Not only did it move, the faucet handle spun freely. It made four or five complete revolutions.

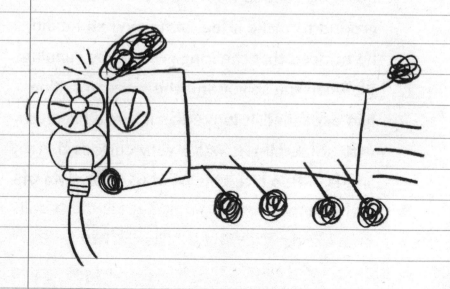

Staggering a bit to regain his balance, Poo-Poo joined Karen close to the spigot to observe. The water still dripped, but not a whole lot more than before—and certainly not as much as they thought it would after spinning around so many times.

"Nothing really happened," said Karen. "Strange."

Poo-Poo rubbed his head a bit on the ground to make it feel better. When he did, he noticed that the long green tube running between the spigot and the water machine had expanded. It looked as if it had filled up with something. It was a very curious thing, and Poo-Poo lifted his head to inform Karen about it.

Except he didn't get the chance.

Do you know why he didn't get the chance?

It's because he was interrupted by Mutt and Stripes.

You see, way out in the yard at that exact moment they both screamed at the top of their lungs, "WATER ATTACK!! WATER ATTACK!! WATER ATTACK!!"

The sprinkler had burst to life. It shot streams and sprays of water at full blast in every direction. Mutt and Stripes jumped up and down to get away from the watery onslaught. Every time they went one way to escape, the water machine changed its shooting direction. They ran in and out of the water sprays like maniacs. They bumped into each other, lost their footing in the wet grass, and generally did everything except get away.

Stick Dog, who had not tried to nudge himself closer and closer to the dripping sprinkler like the others, was a safe distance away. He had been sprayed a

couple of times at the very start but simply
backed away a few steps to be completely
out of range. He sat on his hind legs to
observe Stripes and Mutt frantically leaping

and smashing about. He found it both
fascinating and amusing that they dashed
in and out of the water sprays just like
the three little humans had done minutes
earlier.

Now, to Mutt and Stripes it seemed as if they had been caught in the torturing water sprays for an eternity. But, in truth, it was only several seconds. During those several seconds, Stick Dog noticed the pattern and rhythm of the water machine. When the time was right and there was a brief opportunity for them to escape, he called to his friends.

"Mutt, Stripes! Over here," he yelled. He watched and timed the movement of the water patterns. "Now!"

That was all they needed to hear. Blinking the wetness from their eyes, Mutt and Stripes made for the direction of Stick Dog's voice as fast as they could. They sprinted and hurtled across the lawn. They quickly reached Stick Dog, sliding and stumbling to a stop at his side—safely out of reach of the still-spraying water.

By this time, Karen and Poo-Poo had arrived as well. They had carefully circumnavigated the shooting water.

"I told you it was a water-attacking machine," panted Stripes. "That thing's a monster. Why did that happen?! Why did it just come to life like that?!"

Karen glanced at Poo-Poo. Poo-Poo looked at Karen. Stick Dog stared at them both.

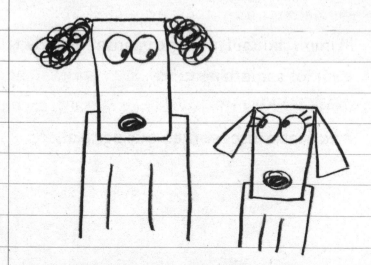

Mutt continued to try to work the sock strings out from between his teeth.

"Why, Stick Dog?" Stripes asked. She was only now beginning to catch her breath. "Why did that monster come to life and attack?"

Stick Dog had a pretty good idea about what had happened. The exchanged glances between Poo-Poo and Karen only confirmed his suspicions. He didn't want Stripes to get mad at them. But Stick Dog didn't want to lie. He really didn't like lying.

"Umm," he said, trying to pause for time to think of something to say.

And that pause worked out perfectly.

That's because, at that precise moment, a loud voice bellowed out of the house that the three little humans had entered.

"Didn't I tell you kids to turn off the sprinkler when you were done?!" an older human voice yelled from the house. The dogs could all hear it booming out of the open windows.

"We did," answered a younger human voice.

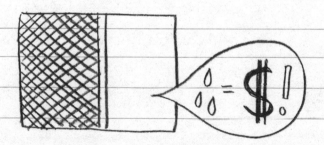

"Well, somehow it has *magically* turned itself back on and is running up the water bill," the adult yelled back. You could tell by the tone of his voice that he didn't really believe in magic. "Get back out there and turn it off."

"All right," the little human voice called. "Come on, you guys. Let's go turn it off. *Again.*"

That was all Stick Dog needed to hear.

"The humans are coming," he said urgently. "We have to get out of here."

Chapter 6

IT'S TOTALLY ANNOYING

They ran as fast as they could between the house with the water-attacking machine and the one with the badminton net. There, the dogs found several large lilac bushes arranged in a circle. The open space in the center of the bushes was mainly occupied by a big green metal

box. There was still, however, plenty of space for the dogs to comfortably duck for cover.

"Stick Dog?" Stripes asked a little nervously. She leaned gingerly against the metal box, not quite sure what to make of it. "What is this big green thing? Is it dangerous?"

Stick Dog had seen boxes like this one before. It was large and had a screen covering three of its sides. On the side without the screen, this one had a sticker that read "Cool Breeze AC." Stick Dog knew this type of box had a big fan inside that sometimes blew out warm air—and made the box shake and vibrate. It was not vibrating now though, and Stick Dog thought it was a safe place to hide— especially since it was surrounded by lilac bushes.

"I think it's fine," replied Stick Dog. He was secretly thankful that Stripes no longer wanted to know why the water machine came alive just a few minutes earlier. "I don't think it's dangerous."

This made Stripes feel better, and she leaned more fully against the side of the box.

"I've seen those things around in yards a lot," Karen explained. "Humans grow plants around them to conceal them, I think."

"It makes a great hiding place," Mutt commented, turning his head to check out the surroundings.

"Oh, yeah. They're really nice hiding spots," Karen confirmed. "I always mark my territory whenever I find one."

At this, Stripes jumped immediately to her feet and lost all contact with the big green metal box. "You mean I was leaning where you—" she began to exclaim.

But Karen cut her off. "No, no! Not this particular one. Just similar ones in the neighborhood is all."

"You're sure?" Stripes asked.

"I'm sure."

Stripes then relaxed and leaned against the metal box again.

After the excitement of the water-attacking machine and the race to this hiding spot, they all calmed down a good bit. This respite did little to quench their thirst on this hot, hot day, however. And it was only a few minutes before Mutt said, "I'm still thirsty."

Poo-Poo, Stripes, and Karen immediately all said, "Me too!"

Stick Dog nodded his head and looked at the sky. There was not even a hint of relief in sight. There was not a single cloud. There was not the slightest breeze. And dusk was still hours away.

"What can we do, Stick Dog?" Mutt asked.

"We came all this way," said Stick Dog. "We might as well keep looking for another drinking source. Maybe we can find some more puddles or something. But before that, let's do our best to relax here in this nice safe spot. Try not to think about being thirsty. Close your eyes and put your minds elsewhere."

Mutt, Karen, Stripes, and Poo-Poo all closed their eyes.

Stick Dog watched them.

In nine seconds, Poo-Poo said, "I'm still thirsty."

Stick Dog tried again. "Come on, now. You can do it. Just relax and think of something else."

Again they all closed their eyes as Stick Dog watched.

 In seven seconds, Stripes said, "I can't think of anything."

"Shh," Stick Dog encouraged. "Try a little harder."

In twelve seconds, Karen said, "I put my thoughts elsewhere, Stick Dog, like you said. So I went for an imaginary walk in the woods. And while I was walking, I had to cross the creek. And that dumb creek was full of water, and now I'm thirsty again!"

They all opened their eyes and stared at Stick Dog to await further instructions.

Stick Dog tried something else.

"Let's all concentrate on something together," he suggested. "I can hear some music off in the distance. Can you hear that? Let's all listen to it with our eyes closed."

In six seconds, Mutt said, "That's the most annoying music I've ever heard."

"Shh," said Stick Dog.

After another eight seconds, Karen added, "It's *totally* annoying."

"Shh."

After eleven seconds, Poo-Poo said, "And it's getting closer!"

They all opened their eyes again when they realized Poo-Poo was right: The music was, in fact, growing louder and louder. It was as if the music was moving toward them.

All the dogs—even Stick Dog—stood up and pointed their noses toward where the music came from. There was no doubt. The annoying music was getting nearer and nearer.

"This is kind of scaring me," Stripes whispered. The pace of her words picked up as she continued. "I've already been attacked by a water machine today. I don't want to be attacked by an annoying music machine too. Let's get out of here! I don't care how thirsty we are. Let's just go back to Stick Dog's pipe. I'll drink creek water; I don't care."

The nervousness in Stripes's voice had clearly affected the other dogs. They immediately nodded along with her idea.

"I'm sure there's a reasonable explanation," said Stick Dog calmly. As he said this, the music blared quite loudly. The volume of it, however, was now not changing at all. It was as if something had come closer and closer and closer and then stopped—and stopped nearby. Stick Dog asked, "Who wants to go check it out?"

Mutt said, "These strings in between my teeth will, unfortunately, prohibit me from investigating the music source." He quickly sat down and scrunched and unscrunched his mouth in an obvious and valiant attempt to dislodge the offending strings.

Poo-Poo answered next. "I'm a smeller, not a hearer," he said with great dignity and pride.

Stripes provided her excuse next. "I think the water-attacking machine may have temporarily damaged my hearing capabilities," she said. She then leaned her head over to the right side while tapping the left side to demonstrate that there was, indeed, water in her ear.

"No problem, Stripes," said Stick Dog.

"What?" she asked. She straightened up and held a paw to her ear.

"I said, 'No problem,'" Stick Dog repeated.

"Huh?"

"I said—" Stick Dog answered, and stopped himself. Then he said, "The water machine gave your coat a nice rinse. Your spots look great."

"Oh, thank you," Stripes answered quickly, and glanced down at herself. "Thank you very much."

Stick Dog smiled and turned to Karen. She would provide the last excuse, he knew, not to investigate that annoying music.

"Stick Dog?" she asked.

"Yes?"

"I really just don't want to go."

Stick Dog nodded his head in understanding. "I'll go," he said.

With that, he immediately wriggled through the lilac bushes to discover what was making that annoying sound.

He didn't have to go far.

Chapter 7

WHAT'S WEIRD
ABOUT IT?

Stick Dog didn't even need to leave the
safety of the lilac bushes. As soon as he
stuck his head out, he discovered the
source of that annoying music.

It was parked right on the street.

It was one of the strangest trucks Stick
Dog had ever seen. And Stick Dog had seen
quite a few trucks in his day. His pipe was
below Highway 16, after all. And he would
often sit outside it and watch the traffic—

including many trucks—go by on the big highway above.

But he'd never seen one like this before.

It was more square in shape than usual—most trucks were long rectangles. It had many strange features. Stick Dog read two

words—"ICE CREAM"—on the side of
the truck.

He ducked back into the bushes to tell the
others what he saw.

"It's nothing to be afraid of," Stick Dog
began. He wanted to put everybody at ease
right away. "It's just a weird truck parked
out on the street."

"What's weird about it?" Mutt asked.

Stick Dog answered, "Just about everything. It's kind of a strange shape, it has a screened window, and it's decorated with colorful pictures. It also has a shelf that runs along its side. And the music is coming from a strange contraption on the top that looks like a big, metal mouth."

"I have to see this," said Mutt as he began to push his head through the lilac bushes. Stripes, Karen, and Poo-Poo wanted to see too.

They stared out at the truck for nearly a minute and then shimmied backward into the hiding spot.

"You're right, Stick Dog," Mutt said. "That really is a strange truck."

Everyone agreed.

Stripes asked, "What's 'ice cream'?"

Now, we need to pause here for a minute. Just for a little reminder. You remember that the dogs can all read, right? Remember how they read "Peter's Frankfurters" on the side of the cart in the second book? And how they read the address on the pizza box in the third book?

And who says dogs can't read anyway? It's possible. Maybe they just can't read out loud to us in human language. When we all go off to school during the day, maybe our dogs all reach out to the bookshelf and pick out a favorite novel or something. Then when they hear us come back, they shove the book back into its place and lie down

real fast and pretend to be asleep. When we walk in the doorway, they stretch and yawn as if they've been asleep the whole time—when really they've been enjoying a mystery or a dictionary or a comic book.

Think about it. It's possible.

You know what would be really funny? What if you had a dog and that dog could read? And what if when nobody is looking, your dog picks up *this* book and opens it to *this* page and reads all *this*?

And then the dog is like, "Oh, man! We are SO busted! The humans have figured out that we can all read. It says so right here in this book!"

Now, if you ARE a dog who is reading this

right now, I just want to tell you this: Don't worry about it. We won't let the secret out. Please go on reading whenever you want.

It's okay. Go grab a lemon cupcake off the kitchen counter and enjoy the rest of the book.

Anyway, the dogs in this book can definitely read.

"I have no idea what 'ice cream' is," Stick

Dog answered, after giving Stripes's question a moment of thought. "But I do know what ice is—it's real cold, and it turns into delicious water when it melts. It forms on the creek in the wintertime. On a day like this, ice sounds pretty good, doesn't it?"

They all nodded their heads in the blazing-hot sun.

"Let's watch this truck for a few minutes," Stick Dog suggested. "Maybe it will lead us to this 'ice cream' in some way."

Before they could even poke their heads back out of the lilac bushes to investigate further, however, the music stopped abruptly.

And that annoying music was replaced by a sound that brought fear to their hearts.

Chapter 8

RAINBOW PUDDLES

Suddenly, they heard running footsteps everywhere around them.

The footsteps charged from the left and the right, from the back and the front. It was as

if a dozen or more humans had suddenly started running right at them.

Now, the sound of human footsteps is not very scary to you and me.

But that's only to you and me.

To five stray dogs who live on their own, don't trust humans, and are afraid of being caught by them, the sound of many human footsteps converging on their location was about as scary as it gets.

Immediately, Poo-Poo said low and hard, "Somebody has spotted us! We have to get out of here!"

"Where can we go?!" Mutt whispered

urgently. "It sounds like they're everywhere!"

Karen couldn't say anything, but she did spin around and smash her shoulder into Mutt's knee. He barely noticed in all the commotion.

"Hold still, everybody. Stay where you are," Stick Dog whispered. He leaned his head sideways a bit and listened. The footsteps seemed to be going around them and past them—some close by and some farther away. Stick Dog was pretty sure they weren't coming right at them. "I think we're safe here."

"We aren't spotted, after all," sighed Poo-Poo, utter relief in his voice.

"Speak for yourself," Stripes said, pointed at herself, and smiled.

Mutt, Poo-Poo, and Karen groaned.

Stick Dog smiled, but his attention was still focused on the footsteps. They seemed to converge and then halt in a common place some short distance away.

"I think it's safe to look now," he said.

The others, trusting Stick Dog completely, joined him in pushing their heads out through the lilac leaves to have a look.

While they did, Stripes repeated the
previous conversation to herself. She smiled
with great glee as she recited it again.

"Poo-Poo said: 'We aren't spotted.' Then I
said: 'Speak for yourself.'" She giggled and
shook her head, taking great pride in her
outstanding sense of humor. "Stripes, old gal,
that was a classic."

"Shh," Stick Dog whispered. "I want to see
what's going on."

What was going on was some of the strangest behavior by a bunch of humans the dogs had ever seen. A group of about ten humans had gathered around that strange screen window on the side of the truck. They were mostly small humans, but there were a couple of bigger ones too. The music had stopped. The driver had parked the truck and climbed into the back of it, and a few seconds later appeared in the screen window.

That's when the really odd things started. The humans stood in a line at the window and spoke one at a time to the driver. Then the driver completely disappeared for a half minute or so. When he came back, he held a pointed brown cylinder with circles on top of it.

The entire process repeated itself for about five minutes until each human had a pointed cylinder with circles on top of it. Some hung around near the truck, leaning their elbows against the shelf. Others wandered off in different directions.

"What are those things they're holding?" Mutt asked after several minutes of observation.

"That must be 'ice cream,'" answered Stick Dog.

"It's a drink of some kind," said Poo-Poo, joining the conversation.

"A drink?" Stripes asked. "I don't think so. It looks more solid than liquid."

"No, no," Poo-Poo insisted. "It's a liquid; it has to be. See? They're lapping at it with their tongues. You only lap at things that are liquid."

Now Karen expressed her opinion. "Those circle things are liquid, all right. They're dripping every now and then. Liquids drip; solids don't. I agree with Poo-Poo."

"But just look at those circles," Mutt said. "They look solid. If they weren't solid, wouldn't they just run off the sides of those cone-shaped things? They couldn't hold their shape like that if they were liquid. I think Stripes is right. They're solid."

With two of them thinking solid and two of them thinking liquid, it was clearly going to be up to Stick Dog to break the tie. They all turned to him. He had a puzzled look on his face. To the other dogs, this was quite an unusual event. It was not very often that Stick Dog was confused about something. That was especially true when the subject was food.

"You all make perfectly good points," he said. It was difficult to tell, frankly, whether Stick Dog was puzzled by the whole solid-liquid thing— or by the fact that his four friends had all made very valid points.

"So which is it?" Karen asked. "Solid or liquid?"

"Let's go find out," Stick Dog answered simply.

"Are you insane!?" Poo-Poo screamed instantly. Mutt, Karen, and Stripes all backed away from Stick Dog inside that circle of lilac bushes. "There must be a dozen humans out there!

And a big truck! And really, really annoying
music!"

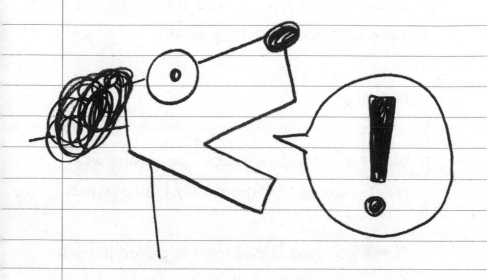

Stick Dog smiled. "The music *has* started
playing again," he said. "And if you listen
carefully, I think it's getting softer and softer.
And if it's getting softer, then the truck
is moving away. That probably means the
humans have moved away too."

This made sense to them. They pushed their heads back through the lilac leaves to survey their surroundings again.

Do you know what they saw?

Nothing.

No humans and no truck. Everything was quiet—except for the slowly fading music.

"Let's go," said Stick Dog. He pulled himself forward through the limbs and leaves of the lilac bushes. He ran to the spot where the truck had been parked, and Poo-Poo, Mutt, Stripes, and Karen followed close behind.

The dogs looked all around for clues about

what the truck and the humans had been doing.

"There's nothing here," said Karen. She sniffed at the pavement. "The only unusual things I see are these small rainbow puddles."

"Rainbow puddles?" asked Stick Dog. He immediately came next to Karen to examine what she had found.

"Yeah, rainbow puddles," she said casually. "It's like the rain cloud that crashed into the earth earlier and was raining upside down. You know, back in that yard? Probably the same thing happened here, except a rainbow crashed into the earth and left these puddles. That's why they're all different colors and stuff."

"Well, that's certainly one explanation," said Stick Dog slowly. "But didn't we discover that the spraying water in that backyard was really from a machine?"

"A water-attacking machine," added Stripes, who, with the others, had now wandered over to investigate the colored puddles as well.

"Oh, right. A water-attacking machine. I remember now." Karen nodded and considered these puddles and their origin a little more. "So these, obviously, came from a rainbow-attacking machine then."

Stick Dog stood very still. He didn't say anything for several seconds. Ultimately, he said, "I can see why you would think that."

"Do you think it's safe to taste them?" asked Mutt.

"I think the drips from the humans' ice cream made these puddles. They were lapping at the ice cream, so we probably can too," said Stick Dog.

That was all the encouragement they needed. Immediately, Poo-Poo, Stripes, Mutt, and Karen lowered their necks and began to probe the small puddles with the tips of their tongues.

Do you remember the first time you

tasted something sweet? Probably not. You were probably too young. Maybe it was a nibble of a cupcake on your first birthday. Or maybe it was a piece of candy on Halloween. Whatever it was, I guarantee the smile that came to your face as your taste buds first awakened to something sweet was exactly the same kind of smile that came to all the dogs' faces.

Immediately, they wanted to share these wonderful, sweet flavors with their friends.

"Try this brown puddle," yelled Mutt. "It's the best, the absolute best! And guess what?! While I was taking a taste, the strings from that old gray sock came loose. They just came right out while I was tasting this amazing brown flavor! The strings are gone, and I've never tasted anything so good. I mean, this is like a miracle puddle or something! A miracle, I tell you."

"Try this yellow one," Stripes panted, before turning quickly to the brown puddle.

"Okay," Mutt said. "We'll switch. But be prepared. If you have something that's bothering you, the miracle puddle is going to make it all better!"

Karen couldn't leave her puddle, despite her friends' urgings. She was lapping at a delicious white puddle.

Poo-Poo was over a blue puddle.

He tasted it ever so carefully—the bright blue was not a typical food color, after all. He dipped the tip of his tongue in. And then he pulled it back quickly. He paused for a moment and closed his eyes to allow that little drop of blue flavor to spread in his mouth. He smiled.

Stick Dog watched all this. He had already tasted a dark-brown puddle of his own and he, like the others, had found a flavor that was utterly scrumptious. But he had noticed Poo-Poo and that strange blue puddle he was tasting. When Poo-Poo, still smiling, opened his eyes, Stick Dog asked him, "What is it? Is it good?"

"Really, really good," Poo-Poo whispered. "And really, really familiar."

"Familiar?"

Poo-Poo nodded and raised his head, staring off into the distance. Lost in thought, he swayed his head a little. "I can see circles, small circles," he said. "They're flavorful and of many different colors. They're hollow in the middle. Yellow, purple, orange, blue. Just circles. They're coated in something— something powdery."

Mutt, Stripes, and Karen had overheard all this. They knew Poo-Poo's descriptions were not to be missed. They left their puddles and came closer to listen.

"I can see a garbage can. It's tipped over," Poo-Poo continued. "A human had thrown out a cereal box. And a lot of those circles had spilled out. And I found them, Stick Dog; I found them. There must have been thirty or forty of those multicolored circles. And I ate them all. They were so sweet. A flavor I'd never tasted before. That's what this small blue puddle tastes like. I'm trying to remember the name. It was something dramatic, elegant, and beautiful. A name for the ages. A name I'd always remember."

"What is it?" asked Mutt, Stripes, and Karen all at once. "What's the name?"

Poo-Poo's eyes flashed open. "Froot Loops!" cried Poo-Poo. "That's what that blue puddle tastes like! Froot Loops! Froot Loops!! Froot Loops!!!"

"Well, I'm glad you remembered," said Stick Dog.

"Me too," Poo-Poo said as a sense of calm came over him. "That would have driven me nuts."

Stick Dog looked both ways down the street. There were no cars or humans visible, but he knew they had to hurry.

"I'd like to take our time here and explore and enjoy all these flavors," Stick Dog said quickly. "But we're way out here in the open. We'd better finish off these little puddles and fast."

There were not that many puddles; they were pretty small, and there were five dogs. So it was only a matter of twenty or thirty seconds before all the different-colored puddles were gone.

"Now what?" Mutt asked. Poo-Poo, Stripes, and Karen all turned toward Stick Dog as well.

"That's easy," he answered. "We follow the truck."

"Follow the truck!?" Stripes exclaimed. "That's impossible. It must be miles away by now! We'll never catch up to it. We're not nearly fast enough!"

Stick Dog calmly held up his front right paw—and Stripes stopped speaking.

Stick Dog pointed down the street. Perhaps only a quarter of a mile away was the strange truck with "ICE CREAM" written on its side. It was stopped like before, and there was a small crowd of humans gathered around it.

Stripes, Poo-Poo, Karen, and Mutt couldn't believe their eyes. It was the exact same truck—and not very far away at all.

Stick Dog repeated, "We follow the truck."

And that's exactly what they did.

CHAPTER 9

DRIPS ARE DRIPPY

What followed over the next hour—and the next mile—was a pattern that Stick Dog came to understand and, more important, predict. The truck stopped three times, and each time the same things happened in the exact same order.

Stick Dog wanted to make sure they had all paid attention. He was beginning to think that maybe, just maybe, he could steer his friends to a greater ice cream reward than just a few small puddles every twenty minutes. This would be, he thought, one of their toughest food-snatching missions ever.

They would deal with many, many humans. The truck itself was large and intimidating. And it was moving.

Stick Dog knew that lots of humans and big, moving vehicles do not make it very easy to grab something to eat. But he also knew something else: he had never tasted anything as sweet and delicious as the small puddles left behind from those ice cream drippings. Not only were they delicious, they were also cold and wet—the perfect combination on this mega-hot day.

He knew it was worth the risk.

After the truck made its third stop—and the third bunch of colored puddles was licked dry—Mutt, Poo-Poo, Karen, and

Stripes prepared to race after it again. They stretched their legs and gathered their energy. But Stick Dog stopped them.

"This isn't working," he said simply.

"What do you mean, Stick Dog?" asked Karen with surprise. "We're tasting some amazing flavors. And we've got it down to a pretty good routine. It seems safe and everything."

Mutt, Stripes, and Poo-Poo wagged their tails in agreement.

"We're getting some great flavors here, that's true," Stick Dog responded. "But the reward isn't worth the effort. I'm getting tired of all this chasing, and at the end, all we get are a few good laps at a few small puddles. We're just getting the tiny drippings from that ice cream. We need more than that. It's delicious—some of the best flavors I've ever tasted, to be honest. But ultimately not very satisfying."

At this, the others all came to the immediate understanding that Stick Dog was right.

"What are we going to do, Stick Dog?" asked Karen.

"We actually need to grab some of that ice cream from the truck," he answered.

"But how?" Mutt asked.

"Let's think about it a minute," said Stick Dog as he led them into the shade of a big oak tree by the side of the road. There were a few smaller trees, bushes, and mailboxes around them, and it was a fairly secure place to decide their plan of action. "We've chased and observed this ice cream truck for a while now. What have we learned so far?"

Karen spoke up first. "I like the light-brown flavor the best! That's what I've learned."

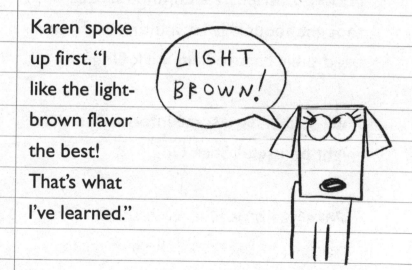

At that, Stripes, Mutt, and Poo-Poo all declared their favorite colors too.

"Okay. Umm, that's good to know," Stick Dog said. "But what have we learned about the whole process? About the pattern of things? About the truck and where it goes and what the driver and the other humans do? What have we learned that will help us get some ice cream?"

Poo-Poo, Stripes, Karen, and Mutt all thought about this for a moment. They tried their best to help Stick Dog.

Mutt said, "I have some information that might be useful, Stick Dog."

"Okay, let's hear it."

"It's really hot out today," Mutt said with satisfaction in his voice.

"Okay, Mutt," Stick Dog said slowly. He panted a little to cool off a bit. "Good observation. I'll remember that. Now what about something that could really help us get some ice cream from that truck? Let's try to be specific."

Karen then said, "Stick Dog, I have something important to say."

"Go ahead."

"I've changed my mind," she said. "I think I like the yellow color the best. Instead of the light brown."

YELLOW!

"Okay, Karen," said Stick Dog. He knew that the ice cream truck was getting farther and farther away—even though it was moving quite slowly. "I'll make a note of that."

Poo-Poo seemed to take this all very seriously. "I have an observation that could help," he said, and pointed to where the truck had been. "The truck is no longer there."

Stick Dog looked at the spot where Poo-Poo pointed. The truck hadn't been there 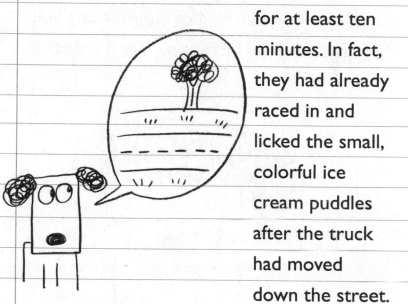 for at least ten minutes. In fact, they had already raced in and licked the small, colorful ice cream puddles after the truck had moved down the street.

"Yes, it's been gone for a little while now," Stick Dog said.

"I just didn't want us all attacking the truck when it's not even there. You know what I mean?" Poo-Poo explained. He then sat back on his hind legs and bumped his front paws against each other five or six times. "That would be kind of foolish, don't you think? We'd all be banging into each other and stuff."

Stick Dog looked back and forth a couple of times between Poo-Poo and the empty space where the truck had been. "Do you really think we would try to attack the truck when it isn't even there?"

Poo-Poo got back on all fours and sort of shuffled a few steps closer to Stick Dog. He lowered his voice to a whisper and said, "Look, Stick Dog. You and I would probably notice. We are the real brains in this group, after all. But I don't know about these other guys. You know what I mean?"

Stick Dog nodded, and Poo-Poo shuffled back to his spot.

"Do you mind if I interrupt, Stick Dog?" asked Karen. She was polite enough to wait until Poo-Poo stopped whispering and returned to his place.

"No. Not at all."

"It's the brown one. That's my favorite," she said. "My mind changed back again. Just thought you should know."

"Okay, Karen," he said. "I'm glad you told me."

"No problem. No problem at all."

Stripes spoke up next. She was a little envious that the others had come up with important observations, and she had worked very hard to come up with one of her own. It wasn't always easy to be surrounded by so many dogs with so many smart ideas. It made her try extra-hard.

"I have an observation to make too, Stick Dog."

"Okay, Stripes. What is it?"

"When I was watching that truck, I think I noticed something really important," she began. "You know how those ice cream drips made those colorful puddles?"

"Mmm-hmm."

"Well, it's about those drips," Stripes continued, but her voice slowed down. It was almost like the pressure got to her a little bit. Now her idea was kind of evaporating out of her mind. She was so concerned about coming up with a great observation. Then she came up with one. And then she got so excited about actually coming up with an idea that she forgot what it was.

"Yes? About the drips?" Stick Dog encouraged.

"Umm, I think, umm. Those drips," Stripes murmured, and waited. She really hoped that great observation would pop back into her mind. But it didn't. So she said, "They're drippy."

Stick Dog stared at Stripes, but not for very long. That's because Karen decided now would be a good time to say something again.

"Stick Dog?"

Stick Dog held up his paw. "Don't tell me," he said. "The yellowish ice cream puddle is now your favorite again, right?"

"No, Mister Furry Pants," Karen said, and smiled. She was pretty happy that Stick Dog hadn't guessed what she was going to say. "I just thought you should know that my mind *hasn't* changed since the last time. Light brown is still my favorite."

Stick Dog closed his eyes and nodded. "Okay," he whispered.

"Wait a minute, wait a minute," Karen said, and snapped her head up and looked off into the distance. Then she lowered her head to look at Stick Dog again. "Yep, that's right. Still light brown. Thought maybe my mind changed again there for a minute. But it didn't."

"Okay," Stick Dog sighed, and addressed them all. "Let's see if I got all the information from you guys that we'll need to get our paws on some ice cream. Here's what we know: Karen's favorite flavor is light brown. It's very hot out today. The ice cream truck is no longer where it was before. And the ice cream drips are drippy. Is that right? Did I forget anything?"

"Nope," answered Mutt with satisfaction. The others seemed pleased with their answers too. "That about sums it up."

"Okay, then," said Stick Dog. He paced a bit, thinking to himself. "I have a couple of observations that might be helpful as well."

"Don't you think the four of us have already covered everything?" asked Poo-Poo.

"Oh yes. Yes," said Stick Dog. "I'm just going to try to fill in a few details, that's all."

"Sounds okay to me," replied Poo-Poo matter-of-factly. He plopped down to listen, as did the others.

"There's definitely a pattern here. And maybe we can take advantage of it by knowing and predicting that pattern," Stick Dog began. He seemed to talk to himself as much as to the others. He listed the order of things the way he remembered them happening. "The driver gets into the truck and turns on the music, and the truck starts moving. It rolls along very slowly for about seven minutes."

All the running and chasing from the previous hour had worn everybody out. Poo-Poo, Stripes, Mutt, and Karen were all now down on their bellies with their chins resting on their front paws. They watched Stick Dog pace back and forth in front of them. It was sort of like watching a gold pocket watch go back and forth when someone is trying to hypnotize you.

"The humans follow the truck on their bikes on the sidewalk. Some of them just walk or run," Stick Dog continued. "The truck stops. The music stops. The driver gets out."

Poo-Poo's eyes closed.

Stick Dog said, "The driver climbs through a door in the back of the truck. A few seconds later he appears in the weird

screen window
to speak to the
humans who have
gathered there."

Mutt's eyes closed.

"One by one he brings each human
the ice cream circles, opens the screen
window, and hands them out. Some
humans stay by the truck and talk as they
lap at the circles. Others wander away
from the truck."

Karen's eyes closed.

"When they all
have their ice
cream, the driver
closes the window

and comes out the back. He walks around
the other side and climbs back in behind
the steering wheel."

Stripes's eyes closed.

"After he gets in, the
annoying music starts,
and the truck slowly
drives away again,"
Stick Dog concluded,
and stopped pacing. He
looked at the others—
who were all now asleep.
"Is that about it? Is that the pattern?"

Nobody answered.

Stick Dog turned away and gave a sudden
loud cough. Without turning back around,

he repeated, "Is that about it? Is that the pattern?"

Everybody sighed, "Mm-hmm."

"Did I forget anything?"

"Hmm-mm."

"Okay," Stick Dog said. "We're going to catch up to that truck and pass it. We're going to try to predict where it will stop next. Then we'll figure out a way to get into that truck and get the ice cream. Got it?"

"Got it," they all sighed as they rose up and stretched.

"Since we rested a little, we should be able to catch up to it pretty easily," Stick Dog commented.

"We weren't resting!" they all said quickly.

"Oh, okay. My mistake," Stick Dog said as he took off.

"I was dreaming of light-brown puddles," Karen whispered to the others before they chased after Stick Dog. "Mmm-mmm. I love the flavor light brown."

Chapter 10

DANCE PARTY

Stick Dog and his friends raced after
the truck with increased energy and
enthusiasm. They knew they were running
toward the potential of a huge and
delicious ice cream treat.

The dogs remained careful even as
they sped along. They scurried through
backyards and the edge of the forest
whenever they could—but they always
stayed on a parallel track with the street.

It was only a matter of several minutes until the dogs caught up with and passed the ice cream truck. The truck, after all, moved quite slowly—and it was now stopped again to serve several more humans some ice cream.

After running past the truck's current parking spot for a few minutes, the dogs slowed and stopped near the street again. In the far distance, they could see where the truck was still parked behind them—and they could see quite a few humans still standing in line there.

"Okay, we have a few minutes," Stick Dog said as he looked in both directions along the street. "He's going to hand out ice cream there for a little while and then drive slowly in this direction. The question is: where will he stop next?"

"Couldn't we just *make* him stop?" Karen asked.

"How would we do that, Karen?" asked Mutt.

"You know, run in front of the truck while he's driving." Karen shrugged. "He's sure to stop when he hits us. When we get hit, the one who is hurt the least could climb

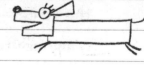

into the truck somehow and grab the ice cream."

Mutt considered this for a moment. "Sounds good. Do you want to just run across the street as the truck goes by or straight at it or what?"

"Oh, I think across is best. That would be more of a surprise—and increase the likelihood of being hit," answered Karen. She then turned to address Stick Dog. "Do you agree, Stick Dog? Do you think running across would be the best way to get hit by the truck?"

Stick Dog had noticed something down the street—a large open space without many houses around. But he wasn't

completely distracted—he still overheard the conversation. He shook his head and said, "We're not going to stop the truck by getting hit by it."

"Why not?" asked Karen, genuinely curious. "You don't think it will work?"

"No, I mean—" he started to say and then stopped himself. His mind was busy working out the details of a possible plan, but he knew he had to stop this idea right away. "I mean, I guess it would work. But I don't think we should get hit by the truck. I think it would hurt. A lot."

"Oh," Karen said. She considered Stick Dog's response for a few seconds. Then she added, "So, it *would* work—you just don't think it *should* work?"

"Umm. Right."

"So it's a great idea. We're just not going to use it."

Stick Dog hesitated in answering, but

ultimately said, "Right."

"I can live with that," Karen said, and nodded. "But I don't know how we're going to get into that truck if we don't make it stop."

While Stick Dog continued to think, Poo-Poo attempted to answer Karen's concerns. He said, "I chase cars and catch them all the time."

"You do?" Karen asked.

"Oh, yeah. It's easy," Poo-Poo replied. He came across as quietly confident on the subject. "You just have to know how to do it, that's all."

Mutt asked, "How do you do it, Poo-Poo?"

"You just have to pick the right car," Poo-Poo explained. He liked the way the others were paying such close attention to him.

Stripes was interested now too. She asked, "Where do you find the right car?"

"Oh, just about anywhere. I find a lot of my car targets at the mall down Highway 16."

Karen observed, "That makes sense. Cars move much slower in a parking lot than on a street. And they don't drive in long, straight lines. They sort of go around in circles—like I do when I'm chasing my tail."

Karen then started chasing her tail.

Poo-Poo didn't seem to notice Karen's comment. He was going on about his car-catching expertise.

"I've caught dozens of them," he continued. "I stalk around behind bumpers or tires or guardrails or whatever. Then I pick my target and pounce. I run full speed until I catch up to that car. It usually only takes a few seconds and then—BAM!—I run right into it headfirst. But you know, that doesn't bother me too much."

"You really do that, Poo-Poo?" Mutt asked.

"Sure. I really teach those things a lesson. No car gets the better of old Mr. Poo-Poo."

"Wow!" Karen panted. She was no longer chasing her tail. She hadn't caught it. "I had no idea you were such a good car chaser, Poo-Poo."

"It just comes naturally to me."

Stick Dog had been listening while also trying to figure out where the truck would stop next. He now joined the conversation.

"Poo-Poo? One question," he said.

"Yes? What is it, Stick Dog?"

"When you chase and catch these cars, are they moving or are they parked?"

"Parked, of course," Poo-Poo answered, and laughed a little to himself. "Who would chase a moving car? That's ridiculous."

While Mutt, Stripes, and Karen groaned, Stick Dog looked back and forth between the street and the parked ice cream truck. He tried to calculate how far the truck would travel once it started to move again—and tried to figure out the kind of place it might stop next. It seemed he was getting closer to a solution.

This whole thing Stick Dog is going through kind of reminds me of word problems in math. I can't stand word problems. Can you?

You know what I mean, right?

Example: You're on a train and you are 60 miles away from the train station. The train is going 20 miles per hour. How long will it take for you to get to the train station?

I had that exact question on a math quiz.

Do you know what my answer was?

I wrote: *I have no idea because I really dislike word problems, and I jumped off the train.*

Unfortunately, I didn't find out how long it took me to get to the train station. I did, however, find out exactly how long it takes me to get from math class to the principal's office.

Anyway, Stick Dog was working this all out while the others talked about stopping the truck. Stripes, it turned out, also had an idea.

"I know how to do it," she said. "See that bridge down the street about halfway to the truck?

They all looked at the bridge.

"Well, we get to the top of that bridge," continued Stripes. "When he drives that truck under the bridge, we jump onto the roof of the truck. While he's driving, we start dancing."

"Dancing?!" Poo-Poo, Karen, and Mutt asked at once.

"Dancing," Stripes confirmed. She turned sideways and shook her hips a little to demonstrate before continuing. "See, the driver will hear our paws banging away above him and wonder what in the world 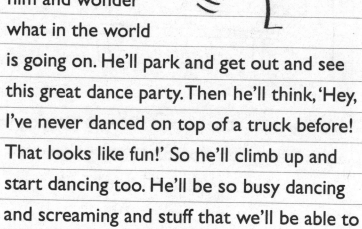 is going on. He'll park and get out and see this great dance party. Then he'll think, 'Hey, I've never danced on top of a truck before! That looks like fun!' So he'll climb up and start dancing too. He'll be so busy dancing and screaming and stuff that we'll be able to

jump off the truck and get all the ice cream
we want while he's still on top."

As soon as Stripes was done explaining her
idea, Mutt, Poo-Poo, and Karen began to
dance. Mutt wriggled his body from front

to back, releasing an old chewed-up tennis ball and three crayons from his fur. Poo-Poo got up on his hind legs, balanced on his toes, and put his front legs out to the side dramatically. And Karen began to turn in a circle.

Karen's dance practice didn't last too long, to be honest. That's because as soon as she started turning in that circle, she spotted her tail and began to chase it again.

She didn't catch it.

Stick Dog, meanwhile, had a great deal of satisfaction on his face. He was beginning to suspect where that truck would stop next. And the more he thought about it, the more certain he felt. He thought that maybe, just maybe, they would be able to get their paws on some ice cream.

But he knew he had to stop the dance party first.

"I just have one issue with your plan," Stick Dog said.

It was as if Stripes had anticipated Stick Dog's objection. "Is it the jumping off the bridge part?" she asked. "Because it's a pretty low bridge."

"No," Stick Dog answered.

"Is it timing the landing on the truck just right?" asked Stripes. "Because remember, it's moving pretty slowly."

"No."

"Is it keeping our balance while we're dancing and the truck is moving and going around curves and stuff?"

"No."

"Then what is it, Stick Dog?" Stripes asked. "Why can't we use my dance-party idea to stop the truck?"

"Listen," he said, and tilted his head slightly. Far down the road, the final customer had been served, and the truck had begun moving slowly toward them again. And the music had started. "I don't think we can dance to that annoying music. And even if we could, I'm sure the driver could not. He doesn't look like he has any rhythm at all."

Stripes frowned and punched her front right paw toward the ground. "Dang it!" she said. "And everything else about the plan would have worked perfectly too. It's just a darn shame."

"It sure is," said Stick Dog as he eyed the slowly approaching ice cream truck. "But right now we need to get moving. I think

I have an idea where that truck is going to stop next."

"You mean we don't have to stop it ourselves?" asked Mutt.

"No, we don't," answered Stick Dog. "Remember, it makes a lot of stops to give humans ice cream."

"Oh, that's right!" exclaimed Mutt. He and the others seemed quite relieved about this.

"Where's it going to stop next, Stick Dog?" asked Stripes.

"Come on, I'll show you," he said, and padded off along the street.

The others followed closely behind—but only after Stripes sighed and said, "I really wanted to show you guys all my nifty dance moves."

Chapter 11

POO-POO FIGURES
IT OUT

There was an open space with a big building
a few minutes' run up the street. And Stick
Dog led them there. It was a school with
plenty of playground equipment and a huge
maple tree that provided a generous area
of shade.

Of course, it was right in the middle of summer, and school was not in session. There were only ten or twelve humans—several small ones and a few large ones—from the neighborhood scattered about the playground. Some were on a set of tall swings, the smallest humans were in a sandbox, and a few more were on a climbing dome.

Stick Dog stopped across the street from the school playground. There was a line of several mailboxes; and Karen, Stripes, Mutt, and Poo-Poo settled safely there as well. Through

the mailbox posts they could see the playground clearly without being detected.

"I think the ice cream truck is going to stop here next," Stick Dog said to the others as he surveyed the entire layout of the playground. There was a large semicircular driveway that entered and exited to the street. The small humans played and climbed and swung within the driveway's semicircle.

"Why do you think the truck will stop here, Stick Dog?" Mutt asked.

"Because there are plenty of humans here who will want ice cream," he answered. He looked down the street to see how far away the ice cream truck was. "The music is getting louder. He's going to be here in just a couple of minutes. I think I know exactly where he's going to park when he gets here."

"Where?" Stripes asked.

"There," Stick Dog said, and pointed. "In the shade beneath that big maple tree. I think he will actually pull into the driveway when he sees that shade. He'll want to stay as cool as possible just like us. If he parks there, we'll have a chance. If he stays on the street, we'll just have to go back to my pipe and the creek. We'll have to be satisfied with the ice cream drips we've already had."

"If he parks there, how are we going to get in the truck and get the ice cream?" asked Mutt.

It was a difficult question to answer, because it would depend both on Stick Dog's understanding of the ice cream truck's regular routine and a great deal of luck.

"When he stops, the humans will go over to the far side of the truck by the school to get their ice cream. They will go to the screen window on that side," Stick Dog explained. "We'll be able to see that the coast is clear from here. When it is, we'll sprint across the street and the playground and find a way into that truck."

Karen, Mutt, Poo-Poo, and Stripes all looked at him.

And I bet you know why, don't you?

It's because Stick Dog usually had more precise step-by-step plans when it came to grabbing some tasty food. This time, however, there was a lot left to chance.

"That's it?" asked Stripes doubtfully. "We hope he parks in the shade? And if he does, we find a way into the truck? I mean, really? Maybe we should go back to my dance-party idea."

"No, no," Stick Dog said, and smiled. "There's more to it than that. If I can get into that truck—"

But it was too late to explain any more. The annoying music was getting louder. The truck was close. Very close.

They all turned to watch it. It was both threatening and inviting. It was a big, moving vehicle—something all the dogs knew could be very dangerous. But they also knew that some of the most delicious flavors they had ever tasted were inside that truck.

"Turn into the driveway," whispered Stick Dog as it passed by slowly. "Turn into the driveway."

TURN.
TURN.
TURN.

The truck slowed down to a near stop.

"Oh no," said Mutt. "It's going to park in the street!"

Stripes, Poo-Poo, and Karen all moaned. After tasting all those puddles made of delicious ice cream drippings, it was terrible to think that was all the ice cream they would ever taste: a few tiny drips.

Stick Dog was still watching. He whispered, "Turn. Turn. Turn."

Then he saw something.

A small light.

A small, blinking light.

It was the ice cream truck's flashing turn signal. The truck pulled slowly into the driveway and parked smack dab in the middle of that huge shady area.

Mutt, Karen, Poo-Poo, and Stripes began to hop and yelp.

"Shh," said Stick Dog. "We have to move as soon as we can. Everybody hold still and watch."

The music stopped. The driver got out. He waved at the humans on the playground and climbed into the back of the truck. Stick Dog knew he was getting ready to give out ice cream.

Most important, every human on the playground began walking—or running—to the other side of the truck. The smaller humans were the first ones out of sight; the larger humans were the last.

Stick Dog said just one thing when the playground was empty.

"Now!"

They looked both ways and then raced
across the street and across the playground.
They passed a swing set, a flagpole, a
climbing dome, and a sandbox on their way.
They stopped near a seesaw right next to
the truck. Panting there, the dogs quickly
considered how to reach the open window.

"Let's just stack up again," Mutt said. He
spread out his legs and lowered his head,

ready to form the base of a dog stack. "It's worked before."

Stick Dog shook his head. "It won't work," he said. "We don't have the time. And I have to be the one who goes in—that's part of the plan. And I'm too heavy to be on top."

They could all hear the happy voices of the humans on the other side as they ordered their ice cream. Karen could see their shoes when she looked underneath the truck.

"We have to hurry!" she exclaimed. "They're moving around over there. They're going to be back soon; I just know it."

"We have a minute. He doesn't serve the ice cream that fast," Stick Dog said. He jerked his head back and forth to find something—anything—that could help him get inside. "I have to get in there."

It was then that Poo-Poo said, "I always find when I'm faced with a particularly perplexing problem that it's best to sit down and think about it. When I do, often a solution will present itself."

Stick Dog looked at him. Considering the absolute urgency of the moment, he really couldn't believe what Poo-Poo had just said. He watched as Poo-Poo sat down on the end of the seesaw. It sank down, bounced

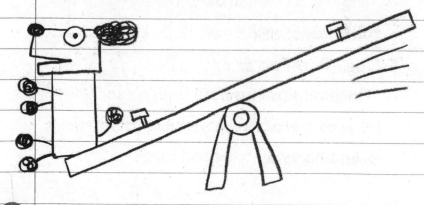

a bit, and stopped against the ground.
Poo-Poo appeared to be deep in thought
already.

In an instant, Stick Dog was by the middle
of the long seesaw board. He stared at it
from one end to the other. He saw the
curved rocking mechanism in the center.
He saw the ends move every time Poo-Poo
shifted his weight.

"Poo-Poo," Stick Dog
said. "Get off there
for a minute, please."

"Not now, Stick
Dog," Poo-Poo said.
"I'm trying to come
up with a way to get you into that truck's
open window."

Stick Dog tried to keep his cool. He knew
one or more of those humans probably had
their ice cream now—and he knew they
would soon return to the playground to lap
at those delicious colored circles.

"You've already found a solution," Stick Dog
said. "But you need to move."

Poo-Poo got up, and Stick Dog quickly took
his place at the end of the seesaw. He didn't
sit down but stood firmly with his legs
spread out as much as he could for balance.
Stick Dog turned his head over his shoulder
to address the others. "You guys climb on
the other end of the board. Quickly!"

There was no hesitation. The others didn't
know what Stick Dog was up to—but
they could tell he had solved the problem.

Stripes was the first up. She jumped to the center of the seesaw and walked to the end opposite Stick Dog. Stick Dog began to rise off the ground immediately. Then Mutt climbed on and walked toward Stripes and sat right next to her. Stick Dog rose even farther into the air. With one end almost touching the ground now, Karen was able to step up onto the board easily between Stripes's legs. It was the little bit of extra weight they needed.

Stick Dog rose as high as the board would lift him—almost to the exact height of the truck's window. He crouched down a little and calculated the distance and trajectory he would need. After estimating the jumping angle necessary, Stick Dog narrowed his eyes and clenched his teeth.

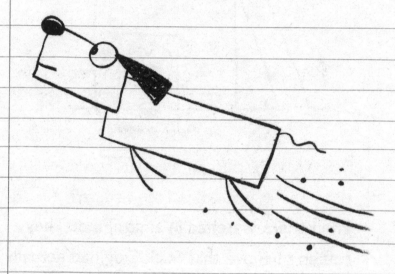

And leaped.

He flew straight through the middle of that truck's window, barely brushing the fur on

his back against the top of the window
frame.

He was in.

The others watched in amazement. They
couldn't believe that Stick Dog had actually
made it into the truck.

Poo-Poo looked at Mutt, Stripes, and

Karen, who had all stepped off the seesaw now. He shrugged his shoulders and said, "I told you I'd figure it out."

Stick Dog propped himself up in the window to talk to the others.

"You guys go hide now! Fast!" He talked quickly and glanced all around to make certain no human had come back yet. "When the truck starts moving, follow it from a safe distance. I'll take it from here."

The others heard the urgency in his voice and saw the controlled panic on his face. They hid—and hid fast.

Stripes ran to the flagpole and hid behind it. Mutt ran to the climbing dome, stooped

low on the ground under it, and covered one eye with a paw. Poo-Poo hid behind a swing. Karen sprinted toward the sandbox, jumped nine inches into the air, and plummeted down into the sand pile, burying herself the best she could.

Stick Dog watched his friends find their hiding places.

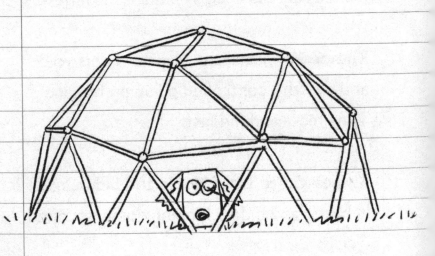

Unfortunately, he could see them all quite clearly. He waved frantically at them and pointed across the street to the mailboxes where they had hidden before. Poo-Poo, Mutt, Karen, and Stripes all understood his motions instantly and raced across the street to their previous hiding place.

Knowing they were safe, Stick Dog turned his body around to look and listen out the truck's windows.

He knew he was on his own now.

What he didn't know was this: he was
about to be seen by a human.

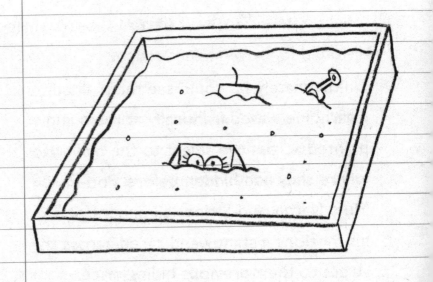

Chapter 12

WOGGY!

Stick Dog stretched out across the long bench seat in the front part of the truck. He listened for two distinct sounds.

First, he wanted to hear the screen window slide shut. He knew that would mean the driver was done serving ice cream to the other humans.

Second, he would hear the driver climb out and close the back door. That would mean, Stick Dog knew, that the driver was about to return to climb into the truck and drive away.

It was then that Stick Dog would need to put the rest of his ice cream—snatching plan into action. He nodded his head backward, flopping his ears back a bit to hear even better. He looked up and out of the passenger-side window and listened. There were fewer human voices with every minute that passed.

Finally, there was just one voice left. It was female and sounded like a large human. "I'll just take a vanilla cone for me and my doodlebug here."

"Coming right up" was the answer that Stick Dog heard.

He also heard the large female human pacing a little bit outside the truck as she waited. The steps seemed to come closer, and Stick Dog crouched down even lower. He listened and stared up out of that window.

Then a small human stared right at him through that window and yelled, "Woggy!" The little human began bouncing up and down. Stick Dog could see a larger human arm holding the tiny human.

And the tiny human pointed at him and exclaimed, "Woggy! Woggy! WOGGY!!" louder and louder.

Stick Dog instinctively held his paw up to his mouth to try to hush the tiny human.

This had an enormous impact.

It started screaming, "WOGGY! WOGGY!! WOGGY!!!" and bounced even more wildly in the big human's arms.

"Yes, yes, I know. You're a little doggy," the big female human said in a calming voice. "And the little doggy is going to get an ice cream cone, don't worry. But calm down. You're going to jump right out of my arms."

With that, the tiny human was gone.

Stick Dog panted his
relief and heard the
big female hand some
coins to the ice cream
man. There were no
more voices near the
truck. All the humans
had returned to the
playground to eat their sweet treats. Stick
Dog heard the screen window slide shut.
The truck vibrated. He guessed the man
had just stepped out from the back of the
truck. Two seconds later the back door
slammed shut.

The man was returning.

And Stick Dog knew he had to get out—
fast.

He reached out the passenger-side window
as far as he could with his front paws. For a
split second, sheer panic coursed through
his body. His paws found nothing but air.

But then, with extra stretching effort, they scratched against metal—the shelf that ran along the side. Using his front paws to balance on that shelf, Stick Dog lifted his back legs onto the lower edge of the passenger-side window. He closed his eyes, shifted his weight forward, and pushed hard with his back legs.

For the shortest instant, he didn't know if he would keep his balance or fall down to the blacktop. He leaned in toward the truck, scooted his legs forward, and got all four paws onto the shelf. He stood there for a moment to rebalance his body on the slick metal shelf.

But only for a moment.

He heard the driver's door open and felt the truck shake as the man sat down behind the steering wheel. He heard the annoying music start blaring above him. He felt the truck shimmy as the driver turned on the engine.

Stick Dog took three steps on the shelf until he was at the screen window on the side of the truck.

He pushed it open with his nose.

He squeezed himself in and fell down to the floor in the back of the truck.

Stick Dog stood up and felt the truck begin to move. He had never been in a vehicle before, and he leaned back and forth and

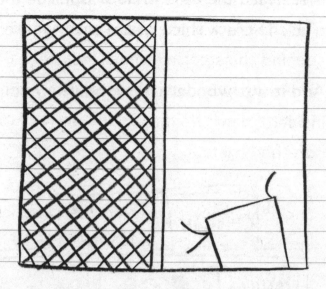

bumped into things until he got used to it. What he bumped into were boxes and boxes filled with cartons and cartons of ice cream.

He sat down for a moment as the ice cream truck rolled slowly out of the school driveway and onto the street.

For seventeen seconds, Stick Dog just sat

there. He had made it. He was inside the
truck. There was ice cream everywhere.

And it was wonderfully, wonderfully cold
inside.

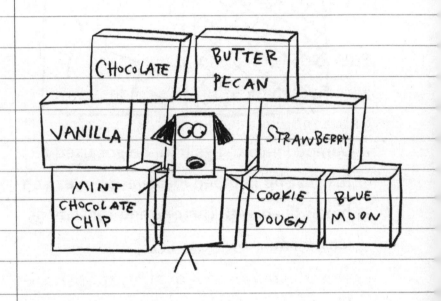

Chapter 13

KAREN TACKLES STICK DOG

Stick Dog took pleasure in his accomplishment—and the coldness—for only a moment. He knew it was just a matter of time—about seven minutes or so—until the truck stopped again. When it did, the driver would come immediately to the back of the truck to start serving ice cream to a new bunch of humans. Stick Dog would be caught for sure if he didn't hurry.

He began to open the flaps of several of the cardboard boxes. Inside each box were six large, circular cartons of ice cream.

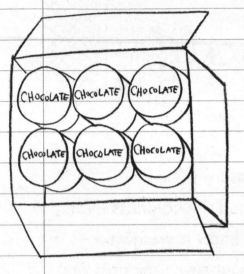

He pulled out several of the cartons. He saw words that he didn't recognize— "chocolate," "vanilla," "mint chocolate chip," "blue moon," "butter pecan," "cookie dough"—but spent absolutely no time considering them.

He pushed one of the boxes beneath the screen window and climbed on top of it. There, he bent down, grasped a circular carton by the lid with his mouth, and pulled it up. He pushed carton after carton out the open screen window. He heard them

PLOP! when they landed on the street. After the seventh or eighth ice cream carton, Stick Dog stretched forward and leaned his head out the screen window to look behind the truck.

VANILLA

He could see Mutt, Stripes, Karen, and Poo-Poo as they ran along the sidewalk. Whenever they saw a carton roll along the blacktop, one of them would check for traffic and then scoot out into the street to push it to the side with their nose.

Stick Dog retrieved a few more cartons of ice cream and pushed them out the screen window in the same manner. He had lost count, but he knew he must have pushed close to a dozen cartons out to the street. And while he had lost track of how many cartons he had pushed out, he had not lost track of the time.

That truck would stop again pretty soon.

It was time to leave. It was time to jump out.

Stick Dog climbed up on the box and pushed his head out the screen window. He looked forward down the road. He needed to find a soft landing spot—and soon.

He knew it would hurt to jump out. But the truck was moving quite slowly, and he thought that with a nice, grassy landing spot, he might get by with just some scrapes and bruises. He considered such things a small price to pay for the giant ice cream feast he and his friends were about to enjoy.

A little bit ahead he could see a nice patch of grass to the side.

He pulled himself fully up to the top of the box, glanced around for humans, and then pushed his shoulders through the screen window. The soft, grassy patch was getting closer. He was ready to jump.

But he didn't.

Because he couldn't.

There was a sound coming up from behind the ice cream truck on the road. It was louder than even the annoying music.

It was a sound every stray dog feared. And it was a sound that a stray dog who had just snuck into an ice cream truck, snatched several cartons of ice cream, and thrown them out the window to his friends feared more than anything in the world.

It was a police siren.

Stick Dog ducked back into the truck and jumped down to the floor. As he did so, he knocked over the box that he had climbed on.

He knew about police cars. They were fast and loud, with flashing red lights. Big humans in blue uniforms were inside them. They were called policemen. They had loud, booming voices. Most important, Stick Dog knew that policemen who drove around in the loud cars with flashing lights did not like stray dogs.

He and his friends had been chased away from garbage cans, Picasso Park, and the back of the mall a few times by these giant humans in blue uniforms.

For the first time in a long time, Stick Dog was scared.

He was caught in this enclosed space. There was no way out. Stick Dog knew he couldn't hop out the window now. The policeman was too close. He had been stealing food from the ice cream truck. The evidence was behind him down the street. And he had nowhere to go.

The ice cream truck slowed to a stop, and the music stopped playing. Stick Dog could hear the police car stop behind the ice cream truck, spitting gravel across the pavement. He heard a door slam and the heavy footsteps of a policeman approaching the vehicle. He was coming to speak to the driver.

Stick Dog knew what that policeman would say. He would say, "You have an ice cream thief in the back of your truck. I've seen ice cream cartons scattered down the street for the last half mile. I'm going to catch whoever is back there and take him away forever."

That's what the policeman was going to say.

Stick Dog listened as the policeman made his way with thundering steps to the driver's-side window. It was, indeed, a booming voice. Stick Dog could hear it easily through the open screen window even though it was on the opposite side of the truck. And he could hear the driver's softer voice as well.

"Yes, officer?" the ice cream truck driver said. "Was I doing something wrong? I certainly wasn't speeding."

"I have to tell you something," the policeman said in his deep voice.

"Yes? What's that?"

Stick Dog squeezed his eyes shut. He knew what was coming. For that instant before the policeman answered, Stick Dog thought of Poo-Poo, Stripes, Karen, and Mutt. In his mind, he could see them enjoying all that ice cream he had thrown out just minutes ago. It made him feel good to know that all his efforts had paid off for them in such a big, tasty way.

"I have to tell you," the policeman continued, "on a day as hot as this, I could really go for a chocolate cone."

Stick Dog couldn't believe his ears. He was not caught snatching the ice cream. The others either hid it fast or the policeman had just turned from a side street or something. He felt a tremendous sense of relief.

But only for a single second.

That's because a single second later the driver said, "I totally understand, officer. I'll make you one right away."

Stick Dog felt the truck move a bit as the driver got out. And he heard his door slam shut. He was coming around to open the back door to climb in and make the policeman an ice cream treat. In seconds, the back door would open, and the first thing the driver would see would be Stick Dog.

There wasn't even enough time to push the box back and scramble up to the open window. He would be trapped by the driver. And the policeman was right there to help him.

The door handle turned. The door itself cracked open, allowing a sliver of bright sunlight to enter the back of the truck. The door swung halfway open, flooding the truck with light and illuminating Stick Dog right in the middle of the back compartment. He could see the driver's hand on the edge of the door.

Then the policeman called, "Hey, you know what?"

And the driver's hand disappeared as he turned to walk back around the corner of the truck to answer, "What's that?"

It was Stick Dog's one and only chance.

And he took it.

Stick Dog quickly and quietly jumped from the back and ran down the street toward his friends. He heard the policeman's voice as he ran safely away.

"I changed my mind," he said. "Can you make that vanilla?"

Stick Dog didn't look back. He didn't
know if the ice cream man saw him run
down the street or not. He suspected that
he probably had not. It was a good ten
seconds before the driver got back inside
the truck. And in those ten seconds, Stick
Dog had covered an awful lot of ground.

Stick Dog did not stop running. He
wanted to get as far away from that
truck—and that policeman—as he could.

He only slowed and stopped when he
heard this:

"Stick Dog! Over here!"

It was Karen.
She ran out
from a group
of honeysuckle
bushes in a
yard close to
the street. She
sprinted at
him and lunged
at him and
knocked him sideways. "I knew you could
do it! I knew you could!"

Poo-Poo, Mutt, and Stripes all stuck
their heads out from that huge clump of

honeysuckle bushes. They waved and smiled. They had ice cream all over their mouths and faces.

"Come on! This way!" Karen exclaimed.

When Stick Dog pushed through the honeysuckle leaves and flowers, he found that they were in another of those super-secure areas. There was a circle of bushes, a big green metal box, and plenty of room for them all.

And there were eleven cartons of cold, cold ice cream.

The End

Tom Watson lives in Chicago with his wife, daughter, and son. He also has a dog, as you could probably guess. The dog is a Labrador-Newfoundland mix. Tom says he looks like a Labrador with a bad perm. He wanted to name the dog "Put Your Shirt On" (please don't ask why), but he was outvoted by his family. The dog's name is Shadow. Early in his career Tom worked in politics, including a stint as the chief speechwriter for the governor of Ohio. This experience helped him develop the unique storytelling narrative style of the Stick Dog, Stick Cat, and Trouble at Table 5 books. Tom's time in politics also made him realize a very important thing: kids are way smarter than adults. And it's a lot more fun and rewarding to write stories for them than to write speeches for grown-ups.

Visit www.stickdogbooks.com for more fun stuff.

Also available as an ebook.